ACHOO! BANG! CRASH!
THE NOISY ALPHABET
Ross MacDonald

A Neal Porter Book
ROARING BROOK PRESS
Brookfield, Connecticut

For the Noisy Ones

A NEAL PORTER BOOK

Published by Roaring Brook Press
A division of The Millbrook Press, 2 Old New Milford Road, Brookfield, Connecticut 06804

Library of Congress Cataloging-in-Publication Data
MacDonald, Ross.
Achoo! Bang! Crash! : a noisy alphabet / written and illustrated by Ross MacDonald.—1st ed.
p. cm.
"A Neal Porter Book."
Summary: Words about sound and noise illustrate the letters of the alphabet.
1. English language—Onomatopoeic words—Juvenile literature. 2. English language—Alphabet—Juvenile literature.
3. Sounds, Words for—Juvenile literature. [1. Sound. 2. Noise. 3. Alphabet.] I. Title.
PE1597.M33 2003
[E]—dc21   2003009039

ISBN 0-7613-1796-1 (trade edition)
10   9   8   7   6   5   4   3   2   1

ISBN 0-7613-2900-5 (library binding)
10   9   8   7   6   5   4   3   2   1

Printed in the United States of America

First edition

A Note on the Type

All the words in this book, from "Achoo" to "Zoom", were set in 19th-century wood type—type originally used to print early American circus posters, newspaper headlines, theater playbills, and "wanted" posters, among many other things.

This picture shows me setting up some of the type for the "C" page. I arranged it in the bed of a vintage printing press, trying different styles of type and different arrangements until it looked right. I used a different typeface for every word in the book. Only one face was repeated—can you find it?

After I locked the type into the press (so that it wouldn't move or fall over when I printed it) I used a hand roller to apply ink directly onto the type.

Sometimes I used the rollers on the press to ink the type. Then the machine pressed the inked wood type into the paper. The actual type is backwards, but the printed word comes out the right way around. After the words for each letter of the alphabet were printed onto different sheets of paper, I drew and painted each picture directly onto each sheet.

Most of my wood type was manufactured between 1830 and 1890. Wood type was used to print millions of different items, but over the years, as printing technology changed, most of it was thrown out. Still, some type has survived—hidden away in boxes, backrooms, attics, and basements. Sometimes when I find it, many letters are damaged or lost, and I need to carve new ones so that I have a complete set of type.

Today, all of the hand work has gone out of the printing process. Most type is set on computers and digitally transferred to computer-controlled, high-speed printing presses. But for me, nothing beats the look and feel of these slightly battered wooden letters that have told so many stories over the last 170 years, but still have a lot of big, beautiful, noisy words left in them.

Ross MacDonald